The Belly Button Fluff Pixie

Published on behalf of the
Marquis of Fosseway
72 Mountcastle Drive North
Edinburgh. EH8 7SW

By

CreateSpace

FIRST EDITION (US)

Cover design by Philip Nicklin & Amy Houghton

ISBN 978-1-4499717-8-6

Printed and bound by:
CreateSpace

THE BELLY BUTTON FLUFF PIXIE

By

Philip Nicklin

'Stand by to surface!' Ralph commanded, as he let the toy submarine rise up from the bottom of the bath.

Ralph loved bath-time, mainly because in between pretending to wash, he could play with his ships and soldiers. Although some days the time passed so quickly, that before he knew it the water was cold, and a thin milky layer of soap floated across the bath.

'Eh! What's that?' murmured Ralph as he spied a little bit of something sticking out from his belly button.

Gently he removed the soggy object and rolled it around in his fingers.

'It's blue fluff!' he complained. 'That's the fourth time this week!'

'Ralph! I hope your washing up there and not playing!' interrupted his mum with an echoing shout.

'Errrm? No mum, I'm just getting out.' He fibbed casually splashing the water around a bit, so as to give his mum the impression that he was just washing the soap off.

As he stood up to dry himself, Ralph paused for a few seconds to watch the submarine swirling around in the little whirlpool created by the water gushing down the plughole. And much to his surprise, there was the little piece of blue fluff, gently riding the waves trying to avoid being sucked down until the very last minute.

'I wonder why it keeps magically appearing in my belly button?' He thought to himself.

A little while later, whilst Ralph sat munching away on his supper of egg soldiers - nibbling them as slowly as possible to avoid being sent to bed by his mum.

Only one thing played on his mind, it was the blue fluff.

'Mum' he said in a puzzled tone.

'Yes Ralph.' She replied.

'Where does belly button fluff come from, and why is it always blue?'

'That's easy Ralph.' Chuckled his mum.

'It's fluff from the clothes you wear.'

Ralph pondered for a second on her reply.

'That couldn't be true.' He thought, because today he'd been wearing red and the fluff wasn't that colour.

'But why is always blue?' he asked again.

'I don't know Ralph, it just is!' said his mum in an annoyed tone.

'If you don't believe me, go and ask your dad.'

Ralph then suspected that his mum didn't really know, and was now just trying to put him off asking again.

With that he jumped up from his seat and headed towards the front room.

'Cough, cough!' spluttered his mum.

'Haven't you forgotten something Ralph?' she said peering at his plate on the table.

'Whoops!' he replied, rushing back to pick up the dish.

After dipping his plate into the foamy soapsuds rising up like a mountain from the sink, Ralph silently left the kitchen – just in case his mum found him something else to do.

'Daaaaad!' Mumbled Ralph; creeping over to his dad, who was sat by the big bay window reading the evening paper?

'Yes Son!' replied his dad casually flicking the page of his newspaper.

'Where does blue belly button fluff come from?'

On hearing this, Ralph's dad lowered the paper - crumpling it in the process, and in a surprised, chuckling tone asked.

'What was that?'

'Where does blue belly button fluff come from' he repeated.

'Ha, what a strange thing to ask!' laughed his Dad.
'Well I asked mum, and she said it comes from the clothes you wear. But how come when I wear a red jumper, I still end up with blue belly button fluff?' He exclaimed.

'I take it mum sent you to me when you didn't believe her?' inquired his dad with a raised eyebrow.
'Uh-huh' nodded Ralph.

'Well son, this is a mystery that goes back to the beginning of time, and because it only happens to boys, girls don't seem to understand.' he said shaking his head.

'You see Ralph, most people think that you become a man when your about 16, but in truth, as soon as a boy starts getting belly button fluff, the long, rocky road to becoming an adult begins!'

'Ahhh!' replied Ralph.

But then he paused - it was as if somebody had turned a light bulb on in his head. 'So why it is always blue' he asked with a frown.

'That's the mystery Ralph, nobody knows where it comes from, and nobody knows why it is always blue.' His dad answered, raising the paper as if trying to avoid further explanation.

'Humph!' murmured Ralph grumpily. For it now seemed that his dad was also trying to avoid any more questions.

But before he could ask another question, his dad peered around the corner of the paper and said with a wink.
'Even though it is a true wonder of nature as to where belly button fluff comes from son, it's best to believe your mum's version...'

'Cough, cough!' interrupted Ralph's mum.
'Believe my version of what?' she asked searchingly.

'Oh! Hello dear, just telling Ralph that blue belly button fluff comes from the clothes you wear.' He said nudging Ralph.
'That's right!' Ralph nodded in agreement.
'Well then! Now that's settled, it's time for bed Ralph!' She said.
Reluctantly, and like a tortoise racing across the garden, he headed for the door.

But as Ralph climbed the stairs, he still wondered about the belly button fluff and where it came from?

He certainly didn't believe his mum, or his dad for that matter.
'From your clothes mum said, a mystery of time dad said, pah!' he grumbled.

A little while later, as Ralph sat in bed flicking through his comic, all he could think about was the mystery of the belly button fluff.

As the minutes passed, and his little eyes became heavier and heavier, Ralph decided tomorrow was another day and the mystery of belly button fluff could probably wait until then. So after snuggling down under the covers, he gently reached out and flicked the bedside light off - plunging the room into darkness. Slowly but surely, his weary eyes began to droop, and it was not long before he was fast asleep.

Outside, the moon gently rose from under its daytime blanket, and began its slow, steady climb through the night sky - casting strange shadows across the land as it went.

Ralph, who lay like a bear sleeping through winter, did not notice the little bright light that mysteriously floated down from the top corner of the bedroom towards his bed.

'Uhhh?' mumbled Ralph in sleepy surprise, as he felt something suddenly drop onto the bed.
Out of curiosity and with only one eye open, he slowly peeked over the duvet to see what had landed near his feet.
But it was still too dark, even the glow of the outside streetlight sneaking through the curtains was not enough to brighten the end of the bed.

Then...as if by magic, Ralph felt the tread of tiny feet walking along the bed. Peering over the duvet again, but this time, with both eyes wide open. Ralph could now make out the shape of a little person stomping towards him.

A strange tingle shot up his back – for he was now afraid.

As the little creature climbed up onto his stomach, Ralph closed his eyes as tight as he could; praying that whatever this little thing was, it wasn't going to hurt him.

To his surprise, he felt the duvet cover being slowly dragged down.

Trembling with fear, Ralph gripped the cover and held on as tightly as he could.
Only one thought raced through his mind. 'This creature's not going to get me!'

All of a sudden, a strange voice floated its way up to his ears. 'Huh! This childling's a bit of a sleep-fighter, well we'll see about that!' it grumbled.

'What! It can talk? No! That can't be true!' he thought worriedly.
But before Ralph could think anymore about this, the duvet was tugged right out of his hands.

'Wahhhh! Thump!' Was all that could be heard as the little creature disappeared off the foot of the bed - duvet and all?

Without stopping for breath, Ralph flicked on the bedside light, leapt towards end of the bed, and upon seeing a little figure struggling with the duvet reached down and grabbed it with both hands.

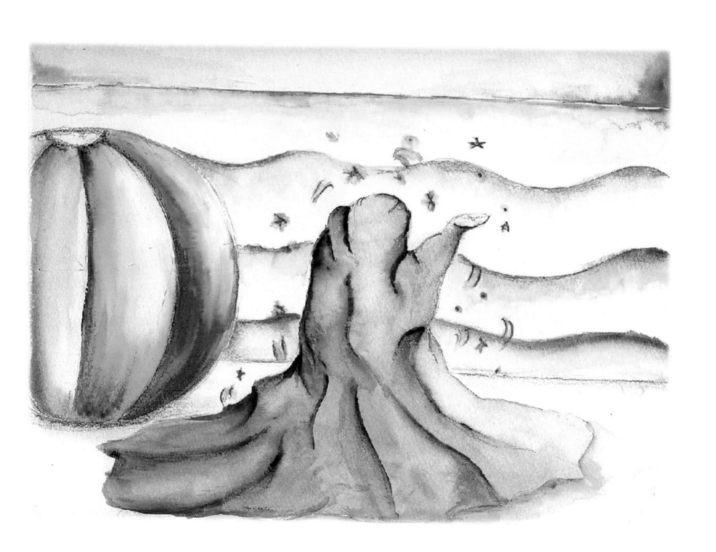

'Ha! Got you!' he shouted.

However, whatever was under the duvet, had not given up the fight just yet.
Left, right, up, down went the cover as the creature tried to escape.

Ralph struggled to hold on as best he could.

Every so often a little hand or foot would emerge from a fold in the cover and then disappear again.

Finally, a little voice emerged from inside the duvet.
'Okay childling, you win, I give up!'

Slowly Ralph reached inside and grabbed the little creature. As he gently unwrapped it, he gasped at what was in front of him.

It was the smallest person Ralph had ever seen.

'You're a fairy!' he blurted nervously.

'No I'm not' replied the creature angrily.

'Yes! You are!' said Ralph. 'I know what a fairy is! Look you have wings, funny little pointed shoes, and a hat made from nut shells!'

'Well obviously you don't!' answered the creature disgusted. 'For I am a Pixie!'

'Pixie, fairy, what's the difference?' said Ralph in a mocking tone.

'Difference!' grumbled the Pixie - who was now ever so annoyed.

'Everybody knows that fairies are girls and pixies are boys!'

'Well I didn't!' shrugged Ralph.

'Well you do now childling!' The Pixie shouted, waving his little fist in the air.

Ralph was taken aback, not only had he caught a pixie, but the little fellow had quite a temper on him.

'Err...I'm sorry Mr. Pixie.' He said.

'By the way, my name's Ralph, what's yours?'

'Why do you want to know childling, you've trapped me now.'
The Pixie snarled.

'What do you mean?' asked Ralph.

'Every pixie knows, that when a childling or their elders catch one of us, they keep us locked up and treat us mean.' grumbled the pixie staring at the floor.

'But I don't want to keep you Mr. Pixie?' replied Ralph. 'I just want to know why you're here, and why you're trying to scare me?'

Upon hearing this, the pixie's head shot up as quick as lightening. 'You don't want to lock me up?' he murmured in surprise.

'No, why would I?' answered Ralph.

'Yippeeeee!' He shouted, launching himself up into the air, and spinning around the bedroom a few times.

As Ralph watched the creature whirring around and around, he noticed tiny bits of fluff, and what could only be described as magic pixie dust float down from the sky.

'Uhhh, that's belly button fluff?' He mumbled reaching out to grab some.

After some seconds of buzzing about, the pixie began to slow. And like a bird coming into land, dropped gracefully downwards, and with a flutter of wings landed upon Ralph's hand.

'What's wrong childling?' asked the pixie looking at Ralph's face and then his hand.
'This fluff, what is it?' he asked the little creature.
'What this?' The pixie replied, picking some up and tossing it into the air.
'Oh that's just cloud fluff!'

'Cloud fluff, but it's the same as I keep finding in my belly button!' blurted a surprised Ralph.

'Oh?' said the Pixie, mischievously looking around the room and pretending as if butter wouldn't melt in his mouth.
'It's you that keeps bringing it, isn't it?' accused Ralph.

'Uhhh…. well yes, but there is a good reason for it!' mumbled the pixie - guiltily rubbing his shoe across Ralph's hand as if trying to brush the fluff away.

Then with a crafty look in his eye, he asked 'But would you like to know where it comes from?'

'Yes! Yes I would!' blurted Ralph excitedly, forgetting that the little creature was still resting on his hand.

'Whooaaa!' screeched the pixie as he was tossed up into the air and over the side of the bed.

'Whoops!' chuckled Ralph covering his mouth.

Peering over the edge, he could now see the little pixie dusting himself off and straightening is acorn hat.

'Are you alright Mr. Pixie?' he asked somewhat innocently.

'Yes!' replied an angry little voice from the depths.
 'Now if you've quite finished waving your arms around, I'll begin the story!'

And with a clip of his wings, the little creature leapt back up onto the bed.

'But, before I begin young Ralph, allow me to introduce myself. In these here parts I am known as Fergus, Pixie of the Seventh Order, and Captain of the Royal Clover Leaf forest.' He said removing his acorn hat and taking a bow.

'Pleased to meet you Fergus?' replied Ralph with raised eyebrows.

'Now then, where shall I begin? Ah yes! First some pixie dust.' said Fergus rummaging around in the little pouch hanging from his belt.

Holding a handful of magical dust to his mouth, Fergus quietly mumbled.
'Spirits of the Clover Leaf Forest brighten the sky, paint me a picture, to show the childling of heaven and belie.' And with that, he gently blew the dust away.

The corner of Ralph's bedroom suddenly exploded into light, bright rainbow colours danced around, shooting stars whizzed about.

'Wow!' muttered Ralph, gently rubbing his eyes just to make sure he wasn't dreaming.

Ever so slowly, the shooting stars started to fade, and the rainbow colours began to settle forming the shape of a TV.

'Look closely.' Fergus said, staring up at Ralph.

Unfortunately Ralph couldn't hear him, for he was mesmerised by the pictures floating across the magical screen.

With a 'click, click, zzzzzzzzzzzzzz!' Fergus whizzed out of Ralph's hand and flew across to the screen.
Pointing he began.

'In the sky young Ralph, there are many clouds, some old and some new.' He said.
'The young one's are white and fluffy, and race about all over the place. The old ones are tired and grey, a bit rough around the edges, and they just lumber across the sky slowly.'

Ralph's could now see the different clouds floating around, some of them even drifted across his head, disappearing of into the wall.

'Now Ralph?' Fergus continued. 'You know that all clouds do, apart from hide the sun and moon, is collect water, which they drop around the place as rain.'

'Err yes!' mumbled Ralph watching little bursts of imaginary rain fall from the sky.

'Well, as a cloud gets older and becomes greyer, it can't drop as much rain as it used to. Instead it just keeps filling up and up, getting heavier and heavier.
Eventually it is so full, and so wet that it turns blue, and that's where we pixies come in.' Said Fergus proudly puffing out his chest.

Ralph could now see pixies buzzing around the tired old clouds, chucking ropes over the top and around them.

'Our job is to catch the old clouds and pull them down to the ground. If we didn't, then they would get really heavy and just drop out of the sky onto people's heads. Which wouldn't be very nice would it?'

'No! Ralph responded with a shake of his head.
'But then what!' he asked impatiently?

'Well! Once we've collected the clouds, we then break them into little pieces, and leave the blue fluff hanging from fences and trees for the animals and birds to collect.' Fergus replied pointing at the screen.

'Why do they do that?' asked Ralph, curiously watching a little bird fly across the room, blue fluff trailing from its beak?

'So they can use it in their homes and nests to keep warm of course!' Replied Fergus bluntly, hoping that there would be no more questions.

'Cool!' said Ralph. As the little pixie fluttered down to land on the bed beside him, the magical screen faded away behind him.

'Ah! But wait a minute Fergus?' he interrupted.
'You still haven't told me why you keep putting it in my belly button?'

'Oh! I thought you'd forgotten about that.' Fergus mumbled sheepishly.

'A long, long time ago, during the reign of King Douhgal of the 3 lakes, there was a mischievous childling, not much older than you. Well this child caught a pixie, and imprisoned him for many moons. That pixie was my great grandfather Eldred' Said Fergus waving his arms about like a teacher.

'In time, great grandfather found a way of escape. But before he did, he decided to play a trick on the boy, just to teach the naughty childling a lesson. Knowing that the childling hated to wash and have baths, great grandfather placed some blue fluff in the childling's belly button.' He said giggling, remembering how the old pixie used to tell the tale. 'When the boy's mum saw this, she grabbed him by the ear, and dragged him down to the river for a good wash.'

'But what's funny about that Fergus?' quizzed Ralph.

'Well!' Fergus chuckled.
'From that day onwards, the childling's mother made him wash in the river every day, sometime two or three times. He became the cleanest childling in the Shire, and boy how he hated it!' he laughed.

In fact, Fergus was laughing so much that he fell over; even Ralph couldn't help joining in. Picturing the face of the angry boy sat in the middle of the river covered in soap.

After they had both stopped, Ralph curiously asked.
'So why do you still do it?'

Fergus scratched his head in deep thought.

'I guess its tradition?' He replied. 'It reminds us of the old ways.'

'Mmmmm?' mumbled Ralph in agreement.

'Well my childling friend! I'm afraid it is time for me to go.' Said Fergus cupping is hand to his ear as if listening to something.
'The birds are beginning to wake, and the moon is going to bed.' He continued, pointing to the windows.

As Ralph looked to the window, true enough he could just make out the rising of the new dawn. Time had flown by so quickly, that he'd missed most of his sleep.

Turning to Fergus he asked in a sad voice.
'Will I see you again?'

'No, I'm afraid not Ralph, but you'll always know that I've been here.' He said with a wink.
'Because there will always be a little bit of blue fluff in your belly-button.'

And with a 'clip, clip' of his tiny wigs, Fergus launched himself up off of the bed and hovered just in front of Ralph.

'Goodbye my childling friend, and remember, tell no-one of me!' He said with a smile.

'Goodbye Fergus.' Ralph replied with a tear in his eye.
And with a whoosh! He was gone.

Ralph never did see Fergus again.

But true enough, every so often he would find a small piece of blue fluff in his bellybutton, and upon doing so would smile to himself. Remembering the night he met Fergus the pixie, and the eternal mystery of blue belly-button fluff came to an end.

The End

Printed in Great Britain
by Amazon

42913921R00020